Fairy Tales

The Magic Porridge Pot

retold by Robert James

Illustrated by Anna C. Leplar

W
FRANKLIN WATTS

First published in 2009 by
Franklin Watts
338 Euston Road
London
NW1 3BH

Franklin Watts Australia
Level 17/207 Kent Street
Sydney
NSW 2000

A CIP catalogue record for this book is available
from the British Library.

ISBN 978 0 7496 8605 5 (hbk)
ISBN 978 0 7496 8611 6 (pbk)

Series Editor: Jackie Hamley
Series Advisor: Dr Barrie Wade
Series Designer: Peter Scoulding

Printed in China

Franklin Watts is a division of
Hachette Children's Books,
an Hachette UK company.
www.hachette.co.uk

Once there was a poor girl
who lived with her mother.
They were often hungry.

One day, when the girl was crying with hunger, an old lady appeared.

"What's the matter?"
she asked.

"I'm hungry," said the girl.

"Well, you shall never be hungry again," said the old lady, taking out a tiny cooking pot.

"Whenever you are
hungry, say to this pot:
'Cook, little pot, cook!'
and it will cook you all
the porridge you could
want," she said.

"When you have enough porridge, say to the pot: 'Stop, little pot, stop!' and the pot will stop cooking."

"Thank you!" said the girl.

The girl took the pot
home to her mother.
"Cook, little pot, cook!"
she said.

And the pot cooked
delicious porridge until
the girl said,
"Stop, little pot, stop!"

13

Her mother was delighted.
They ate delicious porridge
for many weeks.

Then, one day, the girl
went out.

The mother was hungry,
so she said:
"Cook, little pot, cook!"

The pot cooked the
porridge.

But the mother forgot
she had to make it stop!

When the mother looked
back, there was a pile
of porridge on the floor!

Still the pot went
on cooking.

Soon the porridge filled the house and spilled on to the streets.

It flowed through the school and glugged into the playground.

Still the pot went
on cooking.

When the girl returned,
her mother yelled, "Quick!
Make the pot stop!"

"Stop, little pot, stop!" shouted the girl. The pot stopped cooking at last ...

... but the villagers
started eating!

Puzzle 1

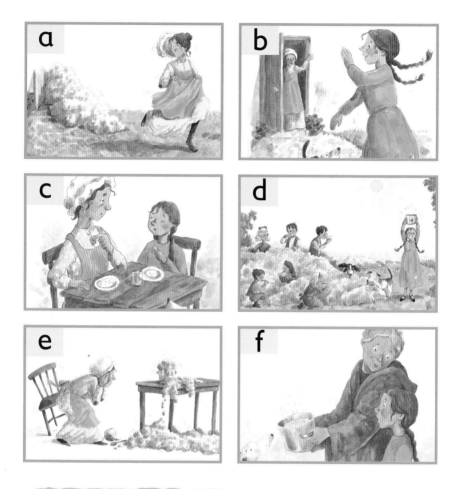

Put these pictures in the correct order.
Now tell the story in your own words.
What different endings can you think of?

Puzzle 2

gentle   polite

rude

horrid   forgetful

mean

kind   generous

nasty

Choose the correct adjectives for each
character. Which adjectives are incorrect?
Turn over to find the answers.

Answers

Puzzle 1

The correct order is: 1c, 2f, 3b, 4e, 5a, 6d

Puzzle 2

Girl: the correct adjectives are gentle, polite

The incorrect adjective is rude

Mother: the correct adjective is forgetful

The incorrect adjectives are horrid, mean

Old lady: the correct adjectives are generous, kind

The incorrect adjective is nasty

Look out for Leapfrog fairy tales:

Cinderella
ISBN 978 0 7496 4228 0

The Three Little Pigs
ISBN 978 0 7496 4227 3

Jack and the Beanstalk
ISBN 978 0 7496 4229 7

The Three Billy Goats Gruff
ISBN 978 0 7496 4226 6

Goldilocks and the Three Bears
ISBN 978 0 7496 4225 9

Little Red Riding Hood
ISBN 978 0 7496 4224 2

Rapunzel
ISBN 978 0 7496 6159 5

Snow White
ISBN 978 0 7496 6161 8

The Emperor's New Clothes
ISBN 978 0 7496 6163 2

The Pied Piper of Hamelin
ISBN 978 0 7496 6164 9

Hansel and Gretel
ISBN 978 0 7496 6162 5

The Sleeping Beauty
ISBN 978 0 7496 6160 1

Rumpelstiltskin
ISBN 978 0 7496 6165 6

The Ugly Duckling
ISBN 978 0 7496 6166 3

Puss in Boots
ISBN 978 0 7496 6167 0

The Frog Prince
ISBN 978 0 7496 6168 7

The Princess and the Pea
ISBN 978 0 7496 6169 4

Dick Whittington
ISBN 978 0 7496 6170 0

The Little Match Girl
ISBN 978 0 7496 6582 1

The Elves and the Shoemaker
ISBN 978 0 7496 6581 4

The Little Mermaid
ISBN 978 0 7496 6583 8

The Little Red Hen
ISBN 978 0 7496 6585 2

The Nightingale
ISBN 978 0 7496 6586 9

Thumbelina
ISBN 978 0 7496 6587 6

The Magic Porridge Pot
ISBN 978 0 7496 8605 5*
ISBN 978 0 7496 8611 6

The Enormous Turnip
ISBN 978 0 7496 8606 2*
ISBN 978 0 7496 8612 3

Chicken Licken
ISBN 978 0 7496 8607 9*
ISBN 978 0 7496 8613 0

The Three Wishes
ISBN 978 0 7496 8608 6*
ISBN 978 0 7496 8614 7

The Big Pancake
ISBN 978 0 7496 8609 3*
ISBN 978 0 7496 8615 4

The Gingerbread Man
ISBN 978 0 7496 8610 9*
ISBN 978 0 7496 8616 1

* hardback

For more Leapfrog books go to: www.franklinwatts.co.uk